CONTENTS

To Mark,
for all your love
and support.
T.C. x

For Kerry, James,
Sam, Joe and Mae,
the cheekiest family
I know.
S.L. x

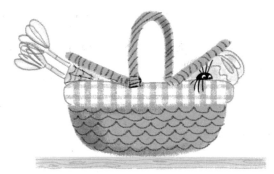

Shifty McGifty and Slippery Sam

don't just make AMAZING cakes. These two brave bakers solve wacky mysteries too! Trouble might be just around the corner but Shifty and Sam are always ready…

The Spooky School

Chapter One

"Spooky. . ." gasped Sam as the Bakemobile pulled up outside St Spectre's boarding school.

Shifty peeped out.

Sam was right. St Spectre's was perched high on a hill, gloomy and dark, like a big black grumpy crow!

They splashed in through the rainy night armed with rolling pins and bowls. They were helping Mr Frogspawn's class bake Halloween treats for a midnight feast later that night.

Inside, they set out their things in the kitchen and the excited pupils scrambled in.

"Hello!" said Shifty, and Sam gave a wave. "Aprons on then!"

Chattering, everyone threw
on an apron and started
baking bread.

"A party's not a party without
sandwiches," said Shifty. "But as
it's Halloween, these ones will be
a little bit . . . different."

As the schoolpups weighed and sieved and stirred, everyone was really careful. Except for one playful little fellow.

"It's snowing!" grinned Alfie, blowing flour everywhere.

"Alfie," Mr Frogspawn warned. "Calm down."

Soon the bread was baked and all the
sandwiches made. But then Sam topped
them off with starry wands and witches' legs
made from striped fondant icing. Their black
liquorice boots stuck up in the air, as if the
witches had dived into the bread.

"Look!" beamed Bella. She pointed a paw.
"He's made sand**witches**!"

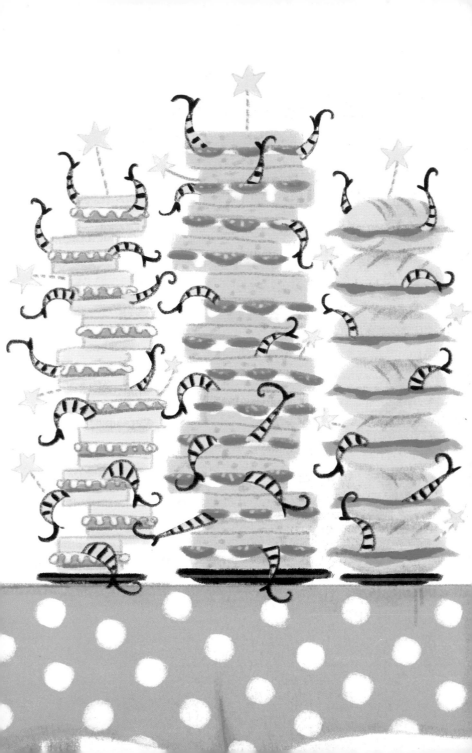

Next they made Creepy-Crawly Cupcakes with popping-candy icing on top. As they added little jelly spiders and bugs, the rainstorm outside rattled the windows.

"It's turning quite nasty," Shifty said.

"Yippee!" Bella cheered. "I hope it thunders – then we might see . . . a ghost."

"A ghost??" Sam shuddered.

"A ghost!" Bella nodded. "Out in the garden there's this old twisted oak tree. And if lightning strikes it – on Halloween – then the Lightning Strike will come and get you!"

"The L-lightning S-strike??" stuttered Shifty and Sam.

"He's a ghost-dog!" Alfie smiled. "He's in my *Book of Spooky Legends*. He's meant to be as fast as lightning, and as wispy-white as clouds. And he's meant to have a really wicked bite!"

THE LIGHTNING STRIKE!

"Oh – that's probably just a made-up story," said Shifty, in case the rest of the class were getting scared. But they all looked fit to burst with excitement.

"Oh, no it's not!" they cried.

Shifty and Sam tried NOT to think of ghosts as they carried on with their baking.

Next they all made Pumpkin Pasties. Then Goblin Gobstoppers. Then Totally Terrifying Trifles that bubbled like volcanos. But the final treat they made was very ghostie – Spook-Pops.

Spook-Pops were little ghosts on sticks – like lollipops, but made from candyfloss.

Sam filled their candyfloss machine with sugar until candyfloss clouds puffed out of a tube into a big silver bowl. All the pupils watched wide-eyed.

"Wicked!" grinned Alfie.

The candyfloss puffs spun around the bowl like small fluffy rainclouds in the wind. Everyone dipped in their sticks and the candyfloss stuck to them at once.

"Now pat them into ghost shapes," said Shifty.

Then they piped on a little ghost face.

"I'm making mine a ghost-dog!" Alfie nodded.

Now all the party food was taken to the dining room. But before the feast, there were to be games in the hall, and a Halloween fancy-dress disco. So off went the schoolpups to get into their costumes, all boasting that theirs was the spookiest!

"Ahhh," grinned Sam as the door slammed behind them. "Peace at last."

He made a pot of tea and he and Shifty
sat down, feet up, nibbling cupcakes. Shifty
nodded. "Yes, this is the li—"

But he stopped as suddenly a great rumble
of thunder made their tower
of cupcakes wobble.

"What?!" shrieked Sam.
They dashed to the window to
see a huge fork of lightning flash
through the sky and – bang!
"It's . . . hit the . . . twisted old oak tree!"
gasped Sam. If the story was true, then the
wispy-white ghost-dog was coming!
Shifty started to pace.
"Right – listen," he said. "Those pups might
think this ghost is cool but we've got to protect
them – just in case. If it does exist, then . . .
we have to catch it."
"I'm not scared!" squeaked Sam, his knees
knocking.

They needed some special gadgets to help.
So they raced out to the Bakemobile and
Shifty flicked the "secret" kettle switch.

Fwip! All the fridges and ovens spun round
to show screens and dials and switches. The
Bakemobile, when needed, turned into the best
mystery-solving lab around!

"Now for those gadgets," Shifty said.

On a shelf was what looked like a picnic hamper. But inside were all kinds of extraordinary gadgets made from ordinary baking things.

Sam grabbed two pairs of BUN-oculars. These were 3D bun-shaped super-specs that allowed you to see in the dark. If the ghost was roaming through the dark garden they'd certainly spot him with these!

"Then we'll trap him with the Ice Ray,"
Shifty nodded. This was once a normal piping
bag. But now it shot out quick-drying icing
that iced baddies to the spot. Now they were
ready for action, like two brave (baking!)
musketeers.

"All for bun, and bun for all!" they cried.

Chapter Three

They crept back through the garden, BUN-oculars in place.

"There!" cried Sam. "The Lightning Strike!" But no. It was just a big white owl hunting mice.

They searched round the trees. Then peered into bushes. But there was no ghost lurking in the blackberries.

"Let's check the school," Shifty whispered.

Back inside, they peeped into the hall. The disco had started. There were mummies and werewolves. But there was no sign of any disco-dancing ghost!

Next they searched the bedrooms. Then the
bathrooms, the library, the dining room and all
the classrooms.

"No spook," said Shifty.

"Phew!" smiled Sam. "But I'm still not
scared – just saying."

28

That just left the kitchen. They headed
towards it with a spring in their step. But
suddenly Shifty stopped in his tracks.

He tugged Sam's arm and Sam froze too.
"Uh-oh. . ."

There he was! The
Lightning Strike was legging it
down the corridor. He was just like
the legend said, wispy-white and so fast!

Shifty and Sam hurried behind as quietly
as they could. This was one ghost they would
need to take by surprise.

But the Lightning Strike
whizzed around a corner and
Shifty and Sam lost sight of
him. "Quick," gasped Shifty. He
was getting away! "Sam – change of plan.
We need to Ice Ray him NOW!"

Quickening their pace, they pattered round
the corner and Shifty fired the Ice Ray at once.

"Oh no!"

Instead of hitting the ghost, he'd zapped . . .
Mr Frogspawn instead!

The icing set at supersonic speed, gluing
Mr Frogspawn to the spot. It would soften
eventually but they couldn't wait for that.
Sam pointed as the tip of the ghost-dog's tail
disappeared through the dining room door.
"There!"

"Got him now!" whispered Shifty as they
headed along. The ghost had no idea they
were on to him. And now that he'd gone into
a room they had him trapped.

"Oh, but wait. . ." Shifty's ears drooped.
"Sam, I've just gone and fired the Ice Ray!"
Once fired, it needed time to refill.

"Don't worry," said Sam, now beaming with
pride. "I happen to have an extra something
up my sleeve – follow me!"

Chapter Four

As Shifty and Sam reached the dining room door, a group of schoolpups came dashing down the corridor. It was time for the feast, but—

"Shhh!" whispered Shifty. "Not yet."

They peeped around the door, only to see the Lightning Strike stuffing his face with *cupcakes!*

"Wait – ghosts don't eat *cupcakes!*" exclaimed

Sam. They needed to get to the bottom of this right now.

With that, Sam held up the whisk he had brought.

"So, this is no ordinary whisk," he smiled. "It's my latest gadget – the Whisk-a-Web!"

It had never been tested, but if the Whisk-a-Web worked, it would catch that greedy gobbling ghost in NO time!

He burst into the room.

"Take that, ghost!" cried Sam. The ghost spun round. But before he could escape, Sam turned on the Whisk-a-Web and a web made out of super-sticky toffee came shooting out of its whisks. It landed – smack – on top of the ghost.

"I did it! I got him!" Sam cried.

Cheering, everyone hurried in and Sam marched them across to see.

"Argghh!" moaned the ghost. And as he battled the web, tufts of fluffy white ghost-fur were flying off him everywhere.

Shifty frowned.

"Err . . . ghosts don't moult. Not even ghost-dogs," he said.

"Unless he's NOT a ghost. . .?" muttered Sam.

"I know who he is!" cried Bella.

"I do too!" Mr Frogspawn scowled. He marched in – still caked in icing. . .

"Alfie!"

Setting Alfie free was tasty work as they had to nibble through the web. At last they reached him. But he did look funny, still dotted in clumps of fluffy white stuff.

"What IS this stuff though?" Mr Frogspawn frowned. But Shifty had suddenly worked it out. . .

"It's CANDYFLOSS!"

While Shifty and Sam had been searching for the ghost, cheeky Alfie had sneaked to the kitchen and covered himself in candyfloss.

"I just wanted the spookiest costume," sighed Alfie. "As cool as the Lightning Strike."

Mr Frogspawn tutted.

"But I didn't touch the candyfloss machine," cried Alfie. "I only used the leftover bits. And I'm sorry I – hic! – ate the Creepy-Crawly Cup— hic! hic!"

Sam grinned. The popping-candy on the cupcakes had given this little ghost the hiccups!

Bella got him a glass of pumpkin juice. Alfie gulped it down, and suddenly—

"Buuurrrrrpppp!"

Alfie's hiccups stopped. But now everyone else had caught the giggles. . .

"Fancy thinking there was a *real* ghost," laughed Shifty.

"But I was NEVER scared!" chuckled Sam.

Then they all tucked into the midnight feast, which tasted really wicked!

The
Wacky
Weather
Week

Chapter One

It was Friday afternoon in Shifty and Sam's café and something wasn't right.

"No raspberry doughnuts?" Matilda muttered.

"No upside-down pear cake?" rumbled Rover.

"No gooseberry tart with squirty cream?" Scottie patted his poor teddy's head. "But that's Big-Eared Bob's favourite!"

Shifty and Sam hung their heads.

"But there wasn't any fruit at the market," said Sam. "And we can't make these things without fruit."

"That's right," Shifty nodded. "But next week will be better – you just wait and see! Farmer Burt's apples will be going to market so *next* week we'll make apple puffs!"

Their customers, however, still didn't look happy.

"So are you saying," Lady Woofington sniffed, straightening her diamond tiara, "that we have to put up with . . . with . . . *those* until then?"

She pointed at a plate of horribly plain
biscuits sitting sadly on top of the counter.

"Um. . ." gulped Shifty.

"Err. . ." sighed Sam.

"Plain biscuits," she trilled, "will
not do! WHY was there no fruit
at the market, boys? That's
the question!"

That was a jolly good question too. If *only* Sam and Shifty *knew*. Lady Woofington now swept out of the café, her freshly powdered nose in the air.

"D-don't go!" spluttered Shifty.

"It wasn't *our* fault," sighed Sam.

Sam could hear their other customers muttering too. What if *they* all left as well?

"Do something, Shifty!" whispered Sam.

"Free milkshakes all round!" Shifty cried. They made them in a blink and dished them all out, complete with fancy paper umbrellas.

"Shifty – we must visit the farmers," whispered Sam. "Farmers Button, Bumble and Boom."

They had to find out what had happened to their fruit. Sam loved a good mystery.

Shifty did too.

"You're right," he nodded. "We'll get to the bottom of this!"

Chapter Two

They closed early, jumped in the Bakemobile and zipped to Farmer Button's right away.

Farmer Button had a big marshmallowy face and a smile like a garden gnome. But today he wasn't smiling. Not one bit. . .

"What happened to your raspberries?" Shifty asked. They looked shrivelled, like crispy bacon.

"It happened on Monday," Farmer Button

sighed. "I've never seen sunshine like it. Boiling it was! Just in *my* field though. And the sun shrivelled up all my lovely raspberries!"

Shifty and Sam took him inside and made him a nice cup of tea.

"Never mind," Sam said. "They'll grow again." Then off they went to see the ever-so-nice-but-really-quite-bonkers Farmer Bumble.

Bonkers Farmer Bumble was out in his field wearing wellies and his favourite pyjamas!

"I love me pears, boys. You knows I do!" he twittered. "I eats pears – drinks pears – I even makes pear pals! But no more."

"Why not?" asked Sam.

"Because," said Farmer Bumble, "last Tuesday there was . . . sharks. No – sharks was the week before. Last Tuesday there was – wind. A tornado there was! Just 'ere though. Petunia down the lane got none. Blew all me pears to TIMBUCTOO!"

"Ooh," said Sam, shaking his head. "Poor you!"

Finally they visited Farmer Boom, who was even more grumpy than usual.

"RAIN!" he bellowed. "Blooming buckets of it! Great snivelling waterfalls of WET! Last Wednesday. But it only rained on my blinking farm! Washed away my gooseberries. How DARE it!"

Shifty and Sam left feeling very puzzled.
The weather had been so wacky! Only Farmer
Button had had sizzling sunshine, only Farmer
Bumble had had wind. And only Farmer
Boom had had rain like a walloping waterfall!

"It's almost," said Sam, thinking aloud, "like
someone's been . . . controlling the weather."

"Hang on!" cried Shifty. He looked at Sam. It HAD to be HIM. . .

"Red Rocket!"

Red Rocket was a power-grabbing PEST
who was out for WORLD DOMINATION!
Unfortunately, he was also Shifty and Sam's
next-door neighbour.

When he wasn't hiding out in old, empty
buildings carrying out his devilish plots, Red
Rocket could be found in his "Plotting Shed"
down the bottom of his garden. Here he'd
be scheming and inventing stuff. Shifty and
Sam were sick of it. Because inventions meant
testing. And testing meant explosions. Big,
smoky bangs that splattered Sam's washing in
bits of garden shed and blown-up marigolds!

Worst of all, Red Rocket was so show-offy.
Although, when showing off, he could get
quite *forgetful.* So up until now Shifty and
Sam had outsmarted him.

59

"Shifty, look!" cried Sam, pointing up at the sky. It was blue. Everywhere. Except in one small patch – where great gloomy snow clouds were gathering.

"If I'm not mistaken," Shifty gasped, "those snow clouds are right over Farmer Burt's orchard!"

"He's going to wreck the *apples* next," gulped Sam. "When we've promised our customers apple puffs!"

"Right – follow those snow clouds!" Shifty cried. Where trouble lurked, you were SURE to find Red Rocket. . .

Chapter
Three

They jumped in the van and followed the
snow clouds to Farmer Burt's orchard.

"And look!" cried Sam. A little way off was
an old empty watermill.

On its roof was a cockerel weathervane
made out of twisted wire. But it seemed to be
buzzing very softly.

"Could that be the *aerial*," Shifty said, "that
Red Rocket's controlling the weather with?"

With that, the weathervane slowly turned.
"Let's check inside the mill," said Sam.
"Come on."

They hurried over and crept inside. Then
they checked out every dusty room.
"He's not here," sighed Sam.
"What's that, then?" Shifty whispered.
At the very top of the rickety stairs, a golden
glow seeped under the attic door.

"Looks like we might have found him," Shifty said.

They tiptoed up the attic stairs. Then BURST in through the door. The attic wasn't like the other dusty rooms. It was smart and full of screens and flashy control pads.

"Oh, no you don't!" Shifty cried.

"Oh, yes I DO!" yelled Red Rocket.

65

The red panda leaped from his huge padded chair and puffed out his chest to look BIG.

"Not again," tutted Sam. It always made him look like a teddy!

On his swish desk was the remote control for sending signals to the aerial on the roof. This controller made the weather do *exactly* what he told it to.

"Hand over that remote!" Shifty frowned.

"Make me!" Red Rocket shouted. He jumped towards them, karate-chopping the air. "Hoo! Haa! Yaa! Take that!"

"Show off!" muttered Sam.

Red Rocket glared back. "Doughnut-tum!"

He did a high kick. "And anyway," he boasted, "soon I'll be ruler of the world! First I sent sun. Then wind. Then rain. But that was just practice for what's to come!"

"What?" squeaked Sam.

"Blizzards!" Red Rocket rumbled.

He rubbed his paws together, an evil glint in his eyes.

"So the blizzards will start on that apple farm. Then they'll spread – hmmm, let's think. . .

EVERYWHERE!

And the nose-freezing, ear-numbing snow won't stop till the world gives me oodles of GOLD. So all in all, I'd say . . . well, yeah – go me!"

Shifty dived to capture him, but Red Rocket dodged away. He ran across to a lever on the wall, pulled it and a painting sprang open. Hidden behind it was a steep, swirly chute.

"Oh no!" gasped Sam. "An escape tunnel!"

Red Rocket snatched up a shiny red skateboard. "You won't catch me this time!" he cried. And off down the chute he went with a wave. "Bye, boys!"

"Quick, Sam!" cried Shifty. And he dived down after him.

"Coming!" squeaked Sam. But he stopped. Red Rocket – yet again – had forgotten something because of his showing off!

Sam picked it up.

It was the remote control!

A grin spread across Sam's face.

"So, Red Rocket wants *snow*, does he? Right then!"

Chapter
Four

The chute dumped Sam outside by the van.
Shifty had already started the engine.

"Jump in, Sam!" he cried. "Red Rocket's
escaping!"

"But, Shifty – I've just found—"

"Jump in!"

Still clutching the remote, Sam jumped in.

"But, Shifty—"

"Not now, Sam – I'm trying to catch a

master villain!"

Red Rocket was weaving through the trees on his skateboard, going deeper and deeper into the wood. Shifty tried to follow. But the Bakemobile was too wide to fit through the narrow gaps in the trees.

Finally Shifty pulled up. "Arrgh!" he cried.

Ever-so-politely Sam poked him. "But, Shifty, see – I've got the remote!"

"Well, why didn't you say that before, Sam?!" puffed Shifty. "Jump out!"

Outside, Sam programmed the remote control. The huddle of snow clouds over Farmer Burt's orchard flew across and stopped above the wood.

Then a great white torrent of snow came tumbling down from the sky. It was deep and thick and covered the wood like icing!

Shifty grabbed some
baguettes out of the van and they
attached them to their feet like skis.
That snowfall was bound to have slowed
Red Rocket right down.

They skied deeper and deeper into the
wood, until at last – what should Sam spy,
but . . .

"A snow-panda!"

It was Red Rocket.

He was frozen to the spot!

Now that he was captured, they

could thaw him out. He had LOTS to

say sorry for after all!

On the remote control was a "SUNSHINE" button. Sam pressed it and a big golden sun appeared, melting the snow in seconds.

"Now," frowned Sam, "what do you say for wrecking all that fruit?"

"And for calling Sam a doughnut-tum?" Shifty added.

Red Rocket stood there dripping. He looked really sad.

"I'm so sorry to say . . . I'm . . . NOT SORRY!" he grinned. And suddenly from his pocket Red Rocket whipped out a *different* remote control! Quickly pressing a button, a remote-controlled helicopter came flying in over the trees. From it a rope-ladder dangled down and Red Rocket was up it like a shot!

Before you could blink, he was escaping through the sky.

"Bye,
Doughnut-tum!
Bye, Giraffe-
neck! Oh, and –
pthhhhhhh!"

Shifty and Sam gaped. They hadn't seen that coming! Nor had they seen the pawful of fruit that suddenly shot down out of the sky and landed on their heads – **SPLAT**! Red Rocket must have pinched some of Farmer Button's raspberries before he'd shrivelled up the rest.

"Ha!" Red Rocket sniggered, zooming away. "Serves you right!"

Shifty groaned as sticky raspberry juice trickled off his nose.

But Sam was beaming. This was just what they needed! He scooped up the juice and popped it into his hat.

"Raspberry doughnuts – here we come! Yippee!"

Trouble At the Museum

"Three slices of millionaires' shortbread!" The raccoon slapped his cash on the serving hatch. Sam picked up the cakes and started to put them in a bag.

The Bakemobile was parked in the museum's cobbled courtyard, selling treats as people came and went.

This chubby raccoon and his two friends were wearing

workmen's clothes. But there was something about them that Sam just didn't like. . .

"So, what are you doing here today?" he asked.

"Just jobs!" the raccoon snapped back.

"Changing loo seats and . . . stuff," the scruffy one chipped in.

"Not that it's any of *your* business!" the tallest muttered.

LOO SEATS

Shifty now appeared with a tray of iced-gem biscuits. He sneaked a quick peep at the raccoons. They had tools on their belts – wire-cutters, pliers, even something for cutting through glass. When Shifty and Sam had once been robbers *they* had used tools just like these. . .

"Look! Iced gems!" the tall one smirked. "We love a good gem, we do!"

The others snorted. "Yeah . . . we'll take the lot!"

The raccoons bought the biscuits. Then sniggering among themselves, they slunk into the museum.

"Hmmm. . ." said Sam. "I'm not sure about them. First MILLIONAIRES' shortbread and then iced GEMS. They seem to love money a bit too much."

"Yeah," nodded Shifty. "Do you think they're really workmen?"

Sam gave a shrug.

"Dunno."

"Well," said Shifty, "there's only one way to find out!"

87

He whipped off his hat. "I'm going inside to see what they're up to!" he said. "Sam – you stay here and mind the van."

"But . . . oh," puffed Sam. "You get all the *best* jobs!"

Shifty dished out a pair of walkie-talkies, cunningly disguised as croissants. "We'll keep in touch on these," he said. "Won't be long!"

Chapter Two

The museum was jam-packed with rare and valuable things – vases, paintings, golden cats. Even a collection of fossilised dinosaur poo!

Shifty tracked the raccoons from a safe distance. They were jumpy and kept looking around. Shifty was sure they were up to no good. They were acting just like . . . ROBBERS!

PANOPLOSAURUS POO

He watched as they headed into a toilet. He'd have to go in and check them out! Problem was, they were working in the *ladies'* loo. So for Shifty to go in, he would need to look like . . . a lady.

He looked around. Outside the loo was a hatstand full of coats and hats. Shifty grabbed some ladies' things and put them on.

They were lacy.
And itched.
And his bonnet
smelled of
roses. "Eww!"
said Shifty. But it
simply had to be
done. . .

The sign on the loo door said:

CLOSED FOR REPAIRS

But Shifty trotted in anyway.

"Oi – lady!" The raccoons rounded on him.

"Can't you read?" growled the tall one. "This is CLOSED!"

"But I'm DESPERATE!" squeaked Shifty in a high-pitched, lady's voice.

Tutting, the tall one turned to the others. "Right, lads – out we go for a sec while the lady . . . err – y-you know!" Muttering to themselves, they plodded outside.

"Won't be long, dears!" Shifty trilled after them.

As soon as they'd gone, he darted around searching the place for clues. Anything to prove that these three were up to no good!

But although he peered down every single loo and rifled on top of every tank, Shifty found neither a robbing plan, nor a loot sack. In fact, the only sack he saw was a big brown one labelled: LOO SEATS. Maybe these raccoons really *were* workmen after all...

He was just about to leave empty-handed, when suddenly something caught his eye.

Poking out of a pipe was – Shifty gently pulled it – a long, rolled-up sheet of paper!

"Ah ha!" he said. He was about to unroll it when – **bang! bang! bang!** – a raccoon knocked on the door.

"Hey! You done yet, lady?" he called.

"Um, yes!" squeaked Shifty. "J-just coming!"

He slipped the roll of paper up his sleeve and hurried out.

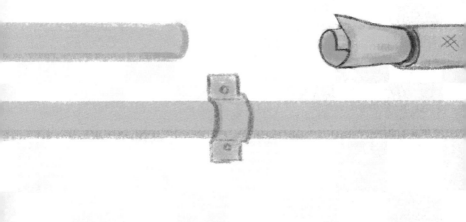

"Thank you!" beamed Shifty. And waving a frilly hanky, he trotted off down the corridor.

Just in time too!

For at that moment, Shifty's walkie-talkie croissant buzzed.

He turned it on and Sam's voice came out – remembering (for once) to use their cool, "on air" code-names. . .

"Doughnut to Baguette. Nothing to report. In fact, I'm BORED here! Over."

"Baguette to Doughnut! LOTS to report!" cried Shifty. "Heading back to base right now!"

Chapter
Three

Back at the van, Sam was waiting for news when a rosy-faced lady hurried up.

"Hello, miss. What can I get you?" asked Sam.

"No – it's *me*, Sam!" Shifty whispered.

Sam leaned over for a closer look. "Pffffff – bonnet!"

Ignoring this, Shifty hurried in. "I *found* something, Sam!"

"Ooh – let's see!"

Sam watched as Shifty whipped out the roll of paper and carefully unrolled it.

"A robbing plan!" gasped Shifty, his eyes wide. "Those raccoons *are* robbers! I knew it!"

"And me! And me! I *knew* it too!" Sam nodded.

The robbing plan showed all the rooms in the museum.

"And look!" Sam pointed. In the Roman Room was a thick arrow under which was scrawled the word: LOOT. So the raccoons were after a stash of Roman coins and jewellery!

"Come on," said Shifty, whipping off his
disguise. "We need to stop them, Sam."

"I'll take the Cupcake-Catapult!" cried Sam.

"Good idea!" nodded Shifty.

They hurried into the museum.

They were going to hide in the Roman
Room until the robbers struck.

Then Sam would bring them down with
their Cupcake-Catapult, which fired a mean
cream cake. It had never yet failed to floor a
robber – not once!

The Roman Room was really busy. Shifty spied two enormous vases and they sneaked inside to hide. Now all they had to do was sit tight and wait.

"Pssst – Sam!" whispered Shifty, peeping out of his vase. "Remember – don't eat ANY cream cakes. We need them all for the Cupcake-Catapult!"

"Sure thing!" Sam whispered back.

They waited.

And waited.

"Where ARE they?" groaned Shifty.

Sam peeped from his vase. "Beats me."

"Sam!" hissed Shifty. "Is that *cream* on your chin?"

"Errr – nope!"

Then, at long last, the raccoons appeared. They were all carrying big brown sacks, but they didn't make a move on the treasure.

In fact, they seemed to be *fixing* things – screwing on wobbly shelves and threading new rope into the barriers.

With that, the boys
lost sight of them as a
group of Dalmatians
passed their vases. Then
out of the blue. . .

Beep! Beep! Beep! An alarm was going off!

"Uh?!" yelled Shifty, jumping out of his vase. Sam scrambled out too, catapult at the ready!

But did all the beeping mean something had been stolen? Or were the alarms just being tested? The crowd seemed most unsure of what to do.

Shifty stood on tiptoe to check the case of treasure. But the room was too crowded.

"Grrr – I can't see a thing!"

"I can!" cried Sam. He had climbed a statue of a Roman emperor and was pointing, wide-eyed, at the door. "There!" Sam yelled. The raccoons were charging out.

"After them!"

Chapter Four

Sam didn't know if the raccoons had pinched anything. But they were *acting* like they had.

They were moving fast, heads down. And their sacks labelled LOO SEATS looked suddenly really heavy!

Shifty and Sam edged through the crowd and hurried out of the door. The raccoons were heading down a corridor lined with posh, gold-framed paintings.

"Oh, no you don't!" shouted Sam. He fired a cream bun after them, followed by two jam tarts. He ended with a giant slice of gooey chocolate mud-cake.

"Take that!"

But the raccoons had seen the cakes coming and ducked. So the very sticky buns hit the paintings instead.

Splat!

Plip-plop!

Spppplurrge…!

Except the chocolate mud-cake had NOT hit a *painting*, but a beefy-looking guard! Covered in goo, he thundered over and yanked Sam up by his crisp white jacket. . .

"OI!"

"I'm so sorry!" squeaked Sam. "I didn't mean to get *you!*"

"Please!" begged Shifty. "Let Sam go!" He could see the raccoons hot-footing it to the stairs leading to the front door.

EXIT

Shifty tried to explain. But the guard wasn't listening. So Shifty had no choice but to custard-pie him – SQUELCH!

The guard dropped
Sam, who scrambled
after Shifty to the top
of the big stairs. Down
in the busy entrance
hall the raccoons were
almost at the door.

"Too late," sighed
Shifty. They couldn't
catch them now.

"We're not!" grinned
Sam. He nudged
Shifty's arm. "What
about 'Hats Away'?!!"

Shifty's eyes lit up.

"Genius, Sam!" They
played that game at
home all the time.

They whisked
off their chefs' hats
and, using them like mats,
swiftly helter-skeltered down the
long polished bannister. . .

"HATS AWAY!"

The raccoons spun round.

"Nooo!" shrieked the tall one. "We ain't got
nothing! STOP!"

But Shifty and Sam *couldn't* stop.

They flew off the end and landed on the
raccoons, bowling them over like skittles! The
raccoons' brown sacks flew from their grip.

"Look!" cried Sam as Roman coins, rings and bracelets tumbled out all over the floor.

"I *knew* it!" cried Shifty. "Those sacks were for LOOT not LOO SEATS!"

As they sat on top of the scowly pile of robbers, police sirens sounded outside. But Sam was more interested in some *millionaires'* shortbread that had fallen from a loot sack too.

"Oh, boy – look – leftover *cake!*" he beamed, wolfing the slice down whole.

The robbers glowered.

"Shame to waste it," shrugged Sam. "Err . . . any iced gems left for pudding?!"